The Mystery of the Wooden Box

AMAZING GRACIE MYSTERIES #1

By Cyrena Shows

Illustrated by Anastasia Yatsunenko

Dragonfly Hill Books, LLC

To my children, Rachel, Claudia, and Leah, who help me keep the wonder of childhood alive.

Table of Contents

Chapter 1 1

Chapter 2 11

Chapter 3 20

Chapter 4 29

Chapter 5 39

Chapter 6 53

Chapter 7 62

Chapter 8 70

Chapter 9 80

Chapter 10 87

Chapter 11 96

Chapter 1

Sprawled out on the living room couch with a cold washcloth on her forehead, Gracie wondered if she still had a fever. A cold bottle of purple Gatorade sweated on the coffee table. Sick with a summer cold during the first week of vacation. Just her luck. She had been staying with her grandmother during the day while her parents worked. Mimi had taken good care of her, but she still didn't feel 100 percent.

Here she was, Amazing Gracie as her dad liked to call her, feeling crummy and tired on a sunny day.

Definitely *not* feeling amazing.

Gracie opened her eyes when she heard the front door open, but she could only mutter "Ump." She knew it was her cousin Beckett, so she closed her eyes again. Beckett lived down the street, and he never knocked on Mimi's door when he came over. Mimi was his grandmother, too, and he spent as much time there as Gracie did during the summer. Because of that, they were best friends.

"Gracie, why're you still laying around? Get up." He picked up her arm and dropped it. She let it flop down to her side as though she had no energy to resist gravity.

"I'm sick, Beckett. I've had a fever for days. I felt awful over the weekend. Mimi says I need to rest and drink fluids."

"Let's check your temperature now," he said. Beckett tossed the washcloth from her forehead.

He picked up the thermometer and held it to her temple. "98.2 degrees. You're fine."

"But I have a cough still." Gracie tried to cough, but it didn't work. Maybe she was better. She looked at him sheepishly. He often joked that she exaggerated things.

"If you don't have a fever," he said, "there's no reason you can't get up and do something." Beckett tugged at her arm, pulling her halfway off the couch.

Though he was a little younger than her, Beckett was stronger—not that Gracie would ever admit that to him.

"Look at that. All my strength is gone," she said.

"No different than any other day." He smirked.

"Are you calling me a weakling?" she asked. Gracie pulled herself back onto the couch.

Beckett grinned. "Yep. Now, get up, Gracie. I'm bored," he whined. "I've played all the video games I can play waiting for you to get better."

That was saying something. Gracie knew that Beckett could play video games all day and night if his dad would let him. He must be *really* bored.

Just then, the two cousins heard a loud rumble outside. They moved to the window, pulling back the lacy sheer curtain to take a better look. Men in blue coveralls unloaded furniture from the back door of a moving truck at the house across the street.

"I wonder who's moving in," muttered Beckett.

"Let's go see!" Forgetting about her malady, Gracie raced out the front door, across the wide front porch, and down the few steps onto Mimi's lawn. Beckett was close behind her. She skidded to a stop at the sidewalk and looked across the street. The new family directed the movers here and there.

The father was a balding man with an impressive mustache. The mother was a thin, wispy woman with a pretty smile who held a baby on her hip. A small white and brown dog yapped and ran around the feet of a tall girl who looked to be around Gracie's age or a little older. Her hair was braided, and she wore a pale blue dress.

Gracie never wore dresses unless she was going to church or when it was a special occasion—like when her mom made her dress up for those family pictures last fall. That was the itchiest dress Gracie had ever put on. After the photoshoot, she hid it in the back of her closet, hoping her mother would never find it and make her wear it to church. Gracie didn't think she could sit through a whole sermon in that itchy dress.

The new girl tossed a tennis ball across the yard, which made the little dog go crazy. He ran after it, tripped over his own feet, rolled across the grass, jumped back up, and attacked the ball.

Gracie smiled. She longed to have a dog of her own, but her parents had refused over and over. She would keep asking, though. She loved animals. Gracie had a pet gerbil at home. She even found a turtle last fall, but she let it go after a few weeks because she thought it missed home. She figured its home was the creek behind her house.

"Let's go introduce ourselves." Gracie looked both ways and then crossed the street with Beckett beside her. She stopped on the sidewalk, staying out of the way of the movers who pulled a dining table from the truck. The dog wagged its tail, ran up to her, and sniffed her sneakers. Gracie held out her hand for him to smell and then scratched the dog's ears.

"Good thing he doesn't bite," Beckett said as he eyed the dog with uncertainty.

"No, Hugo doesn't bite," the girl said.

"What kind is he?" Beckett asked.

"I'm not sure. Some kind of Jack Russell-beagle mix, my mom says. Hugo is a pound rescue."

"Oh, that's great!" Gracie said. Mimi had picked out a cat from the pound to rescue last year. The animals there seemed so lonely and unloved. It made her heart ache to think about it. She wished they could have taken them all home.

Gracie and Beckett bent down to scratch Hugo's ears and neck more vigorously. Hugo seemed to love the attention. He panted with delight, his tongue hanging out of his mouth, and it looked like he was smiling. "You got yourself a good family, huh, boy?"

"He likes you," the girl stated. "I'm Cassidy Green."

Gracie stood up. "I'm Gracie Lane, and this is my cousin Beckett Adams. My mom and his dad are siblings. Our grandmother lives there," Gracie said as she pointed to the house, "and we spend a lot of our summer there."

"I'll see you around, then?"

"Of course!"

"Well, I better get inside. I have a lot of unpacking to do now that all our stuff is here. Nice to meet you." Cassidy smiled, picked up Hugo, and walked inside her house.

Gracie was bursting with excitement. "This is amazing! We have someone new to hang out with that's our age." She tugged on his sleeve as they walked back across the road. "Isn't it amazing, Beckett?"

"Yeah, sure," he said. "Amazing."

Gracie thought she noted sarcasm in Beckett's voice, but she decided to ignore it.

Chapter 2

Gracie ate her oatmeal and bacon at record speed and was out the door before Mimi had the breakfast dishes cleaned. Beckett's dad worked from home, so Beckett slept late every day during the summer. He wouldn't be at Mimi's for at least another hour.

Gracie had given Cassidy a few days to unpack and settle in, but now, she wanted to get to know the new neighbor. When Gracie stepped up to the front door of Cassidy's house, she heard a baby crying—well, actually screaming.

Gracie had second thoughts about disturbing the family so early, and she turned to go. Suddenly, the door opened, and Hugo and Cassidy burst outside.

"Thank goodness you're here. I've got to get out of here," Cassidy said with a sigh. Even little Hugo, wagging his short tail, looked relieved to be outside and away from the crying baby.

"What's going on?" Gracie peered into the house past Cassidy as the door shut.

"Oh, Jameson, that's my little brother, the one screaming like crazy. He's teething and so cranky right now. Mama's trying to get him down for a nap. He keeps us up at night and fusses all day.

Mama says he'll be better soon, but I wish he was already back to his sweet, cuddly self." Cassidy swiped a wavy, brown lock of hair out of her eyes. "I'm glad you came over."

Hugo hopped up and down, trying to get Gracie's attention. She patted his head and tossed him the tennis ball that was lying by the front bushes.

"Want to go around to my backyard? My dad put up a swing back there yesterday."

"Sure." Gracie noticed that Cassidy was in shorts and a t-shirt today instead of a dress.

"We lived in an apartment in the city before, so I've never had my own swing. We went to the park sometimes, but I didn't even have a yard."

Gracie looked at Cassidy with wide-eyed wonder. She couldn't imagine living someplace without a backyard.

"Hugo loves running around out here, too." Hugo had his nose buried in a thick mass of lilies by the wooden fence at the side of the house.

"I've lived in Loblolly my whole life. We actually live outside of town, and I have a huge yard in the country with woods on either side *and* behind my house."

Cassidy blinked. "You live on a farm?"

"No, we don't have a farm. We just live in the country."

Cassidy furrowed her brow and slowly nodded her head as though she understood, but Gracie thought Cassidy looked confused. "Not everyone who lives in the country has livestock or fields of corn or cotton," Gracie explained. "We don't even own a tractor, though when my dad has to cut the grass, I bet he wishes he had a tractor."

Cassidy stopped at a huge oak tree with a wooden swing tied to a tree limb by thick pieces of rope. She beamed proudly.

"This is an amazing swing!" Gracie exclaimed. She hopped onto the swing to try it out. Gracie wouldn't have guessed that their backyard was as big as it was. The tree was near the back of the lot and cast the lawn into deep shade. The lawn was bare in spots under the old tree.

Hugo sniffed around as Gracie and Cassidy took turns pushing each other on the swing.

"Stop that digging, Hugo!" Cassidy said. She shooed him away from a spot where he was clawing at the ground. The girls laughed at his little nose all covered with dirt.

Just then, Gracie noticed Beckett coming around the house. "There you are! I've been looking everywhere for you this morning," he said. He seemed a little annoyed, but he brightened up when he saw the swing.

"Cassidy was showing me the new swing her dad put up."

"Nice. What's Hugo doing?" The little dog had returned to the spot and was digging with all his might.

"Hugo, stop that!" Cassidy ran over and tried to pull the little dog away, but he went right back to digging. Hugo had dug several inches down by that point.

"Hey, what is that?" Beckett squatted down beside the dog and pointed at the hole. Something was visible in the dirt.

"Hugo, move." Cassidy pushed the dog away, and they could see something in the dirt. Beckett and Gracie dug their fingers into the dirt, scooping it away bit by bit.

"What is it?" Cassidy asked, peering over their shoulders.

"It looks like a piece of wood. A dumb piece of wood." Beckett sat back and wiped his brow, leaving a smear of dirt on his sweaty forehead.

Gracie kept digging. Surely, Hugo wouldn't be going crazy over a piece of wood. She got a stick and dug all around it. "No, it's a box. Look, it's square. And there's some type of decoration on top!" Gracie exclaimed.

All three clawed at the box until Beckett got a good grip on the edge and pulled it up out of the earth. It was about the size of a book and three or four inches tall. The top was wood with roses carved into it. It looked old.

"What's in it?" Gracie asked. "Could it be treasure?"

"Maybe it's jewels," Cassidy said.

Beckett gently lifted the top, which was a wooden lid with no hinges. Green velvet material lined the inside. A single metal key lay in the middle of the velvet. It was long and skinny and peculiar-looking.

"That's a key, right?" Beckett asked.

Gracie picked it up and turned it over in her hand. "Yes, but it's not like one I've ever seen."

"Me, either. I wonder how long it's been buried here," Cassidy said, touching the ornate head of the key with her fingertips.

"What does it go to?" Gracie asked.

"Who knows?"

"Why would someone bury it?" Beckett asked. "And are they coming back for it?"

All three looked over their shoulders as if they expected someone to be coming after the wooden box and key at that very second. Gracie gasped, and Beckett hollered and fell back, the wooden box falling from his hand, as a figure loomed over them.

Chapter 3

"Dad! You scared us half to death!" Cassidy giggled. Beckett jumped up and dusted off his shorts, his face red with embarrassment.

"You might want to fill in that hole before your mom sees it," Mr. Green said.

"Yes, sir, we will!" Beckett croaked. He shoveled in the dirt with the side of his sneaker. Cassidy's father didn't seem to notice the box on the ground behind the children. Mr. Green carried his hedge trimmers over to the fence and began shaping the bushes.

"Normally, my mom might have a hissy fit over a hole in the yard, but I think Jameson has her too busy to notice."

Cassidy helped Beckett fill in the hole while Gracie returned the key to the velvet-lined box and closed the lid. They stamped the dirt down, but there was still a sunken spot where the box once was. Cassidy pulled her little brother's plastic slide over to the hole to cover the spot for now.

"Let's take this over to Mimi's and inspect the box closer," said Gracie. The three walked across the street and sat down on the front steps of Mimi's house.

"I think we should put it back in the hole," advised Beckett. "We don't know who it belonged to, and it's not ours to take."

Cassidy frowned. "I don't want to get in trouble..."

"If Cassidy's family bought the house and the lot that the house sits on, then it technically belongs to them now. Right, Cassidy?"

"I think so." Cassidy shrugged.

"Besides, the person who put it here might not even be alive today. It looks ancient."

"We don't even know what it goes to. What good is it to us?" Beckett asked as he stood and leaned against one of the front columns.

"What if it's the key to treasure? Wouldn't you love to get your hands on some treasure? Besides, it's obviously a special key. Have you ever seen a key like this?" Gracie raised her right eyebrow, a habit she paired with challenging someone. "Well, neither have I, so if we can find a unique lock, we can at least try the key. What would that hurt? Beckett, don't you love a good mystery?"

He shrugged. "Sure."

Gracie set the box on the top step and took out the key. "Let's see if Mimi can tell us anything about it."

The three kids went inside and found Mimi squeezing lemons and removing seeds for her famous lemonade.

"Hi, kids. Who've we got here?" Mimi eyed the girl as Cassidy peeked around Beckett.

"This is Cassidy Green. She moved in across the street."

"Nice to meet you. Settling in okay?" Mimi asked.

"Yes, ma'am."

"Good. I'll have to pay a visit and welcome your parents to the neighborhood. I hope you stay for a glass of my lemonade. Not too tart, not too sweet."

"Oh, yeah, it's the best," Gracie chimed in. "Do you know who all has lived in her house before her family moved in, Mimi?"

Mimi's kettle whistled, and she scooted over to turn it off. "Hmmm... let me see. It's been unoccupied for a while." She poured the boiling water into the pitcher already filled with sugar. "Before that, the Bentleys lived there, an older couple who had retired there. The ones who built the house were the Greggs—Melina and her husband George. They built that house when I was dating your Pops. It was rented probably half a dozen times through the years. Why?"

"We were just curious," said Cassidy.

"Mimi, what kind of key is this?" Gracie held up the key.

Mimi pulled her glasses out of her curled hair and placed them on her nose. "That, my dear Grace, is a skeleton key."

"A what?" Eyes wide, Gracie wondered if it was somehow made of bones, and she grimaced. "That's from someone's bones?"

"No, no. This one is brass. In the olden days, skeleton keys were common."

"Did they lock graveyards?" Beckett asked. "Or tombs?"

"No, nothing to do with bones. The name comes from the skinny shape of the key. One key could open many doors in a house. That was a master key, but not all skeleton keys are master keys. Sometimes, they unlocked pieces of furniture, such as desks, cabinets, a wardrobe, or even a steamer trunk. Where did you get it?"

"It's mine," Cassidy said and held out her hand.

Mimi raised her eyebrows, smiled, and dropped it into Cassidy's palm. "That's interesting," she said. "I haven't seen one of those in ages." Mimi added the lemon juice and ice cubes to the pitcher and poured the kids some glasses of lemonade. The kids returned to the front porch.

Beckett and Cassidy sat on the porch swing. Hugo, who had waited outside while the kids were talking to Mimi, now jumped onto the swing and settled down beside Cassidy.

Gracie paced back and forth, ignoring the creaking of the wood underfoot. "Your house isn't old enough to have locks like that key would fit into."

"Definitely not," agreed Cassidy, looking down at the skinny brass key in her hand.

"So maybe it's been buried there a long time, like before that house was built. Maybe even a hundred years. Amazing!" exclaimed Gracie.

Beckett turned the box over and over in his hands, trying to find a clue. He flicked a dried clump of mud off the bottom and said, "Hey, what's this?"

The girls crowded around Beckett to look at the bottom of the box.

"It's a name!" cried Gracie.

Chapter 4

WHITMORE was carved into the wood on the bottom of the box.

"That's a name," Gracie insisted.

"It could be a company name," said Beckett.

"It's the person's name. I can feel it," Gracie said, her green eyes wide with excitement. "Someone named Whitmore must have buried this box under the oak."

"Whitmore? Where have I heard that before?" Beckett frowned and scratched his head as he handed the box to Gracie.

She paced back and forth. "Oh! I know," said Gracie. "Whitmore Pharmacy. My dad used to take me for ice cream there. They took the ice cream part out about two years ago and replaced it with gifts." Gracie frowned like that was the most awful idea anyone had ever had. "Who wants candles and pottery when they're sick? I'd rather have ice cream."

"Mr. Whitmore still works there. I saw him when I went to the pharmacy with my mom. We could ask him about the key and wooden box."

"Beckett, he could take the key and box away from us since it has his name on it. Then, we would never solve the mystery. Don't you want to know what it opens first?"

"Maybe it opens something at the pharmacy," Cassidy suggested.

"Maybe. Cassidy, can I keep the key tonight and see if my dad will drive me over there before we go home?"

"I guess so," Cassidy said, giving up the key as though it were her favorite possession.

"I promise to take good care of it and bring it right back to you tomorrow."

***

That evening, Gracie's dad picked her up after he got off work. She slid into the backseat and buckled up.

"Hey there, Amazing Gracie. Did you have a good day? Do anything interesting?"

"Beckett and I hung out at Cassidy's house. We dug up a treasure!"

"You did? Wow! What was the treasure?"

"We found a skeleton key in a box," she explained. "Mimi says it could go to lots of things, but we haven't found a lock that it fits."

"Well, that's a pretty great treasure anyway. Skeleton keys are becoming rarer these days," he said as he drove through town. Loblolly was a sprawling small southern town with a handful of restaurants, a pretty downtown area with quaint shops, several churches and schools, and a lake. In Gracie's opinion, it was the perfect place to grow up.

"Before we go home, I wondered if you would drive me over to Whitmore Pharmacy. I need..." Gracie paused because she hadn't considered a reason to give her dad for going there. She didn't think he would drive her to the pharmacy just so she could look around to see if an old key would fit into any locks in the building. "Uh, I need to buy Mimi a gift for Grandmother's Day." She sure hoped there was a Grandmother's Day. They had celebrated Mother's Day last month, so why not?

"Well, there's a Grandparent's Day, but it's a couple of months off, if I remember correctly."

"I still think I should buy Mimi a gift. Don't you? After all, she does take good care of me all summer long. She deserves a token of appreciation." Gracie remembered that phrase from some Mother's Day commercial that had overplayed on the television last month. She was very proud of herself for remembering it. She beamed at her dad, and he laughed.

"Okay, Gracie, we can make a quick stop at the pharmacy. I do need to get a refill of my allergy medication, I guess."

"Perfect!" she exclaimed. Gracie patted the key in her pocket. She sure hoped she'd be able to solve this mystery.

Gracie and her dad pulled up in front of Whitmore Pharmacy and parked. Gracie hopped out of the car and went inside the store. The mixture of spicy and flowery smells of the large candle section at the front of the store tickled her nose.

"You look around while I see about getting my allergy meds filled," her dad said with a sniffle. His hay fever had been acting up from cutting grass. He kept saying he was going to hire Beckett to do the weekly job for him, but he hadn't given up the reins of his old lawnmower yet. Gracie suspected her dad liked mowing the grass, despite what it did to his allergies.

"Okay," she said, wandering among the pillows, figurines, pottery, and table linens. Gracie *did* plan to buy Mimi something. She didn't only want to use that as an excuse to come to the pharmacy. What she was looking for, though, was a steam trunk, old cabinet, or desk that had the special kind of lock the skeleton key would fit into. She didn't find anything she thought the key would fit. She was feeling a bit defeated when she noticed a dark hallway that probably led to a back office. Maybe she would find an old desk there.

Should she venture into the back by herself? She didn't want to get into trouble, but her curiosity got the better of her. She had to see what might be back there.

Gracie looked around to see if anyone was watching. Her dad was standing in line talking to another man, and the salesclerks were helping other customers. She made her way quickly to the hallway, hugging the wall and staying in the shadows as she went. She came upon a door on her left. She turned the knob, and the door swung open.

Cyrena Shows

Gracie found herself in a small office with a desk, too modern for the skeleton key in her hand. She also saw a filing cabinet and lots of clutter. Luckily, no one was there. She looked around for a moment but saw no locks that would fit the brass key. She closed the door and ventured further down the hallway, not sure what else might be in the back of the store.

One lone bulb buzzed with electricity above her head. Holding her breath, Gracie opened a door on her right, but it was only a broom closet. The hall turned right and opened into a large storage room. Pallets of boxes were piled in some manner of an organization that she didn't understand. Gracie was sure someone would be back here working, so she tiptoed her way around the mountains of boxes and pallets piled high.

"Maybe there's something back here I can use this key in," Gracie muttered.

Gracie paused, sure she had heard the tick ticking of someone's feet across the concrete of the storage room. She held her breath as she strained to listen, but the pounding of her heart was loud in her ears.

Too loud.

She began to sweat. She should have gotten Beckett to come with her. She turned around, resolved to give up the hunt by herself when she slammed into a wall.

A wall that grabbed her with two strong hands.

Chapter 5

"Ouch!"

"Whoa, there! I almost knocked you down, little girl," a gruff male voice said. She looked up into the gray eyes of old Mr. Whitmore himself!

"I'm sorry," Gracie said. She stepped back from his steadying hands and rubbed her shoulder where she had run into him. "I was looking for the bathroom and got a little lost." She didn't like to lie to him, but she didn't want to get into trouble for wandering around in the back of his store.

Mr. Whitmore smelled of pipe tobacco, and his white hair was a bit disheveled as though he had just taken off a hat. He was a tall, thin man, and he wore a constant frown. She had seen him from time to time behind the counter at the pharmacy when her dad took her to get ice cream. Maybe she should ask him why they took out the ice cream part, though by the way he was scowling at her, she thought better of it and kept her mouth shut.

"Easy to do around here," he said as he peered down at her over his round glasses. "No customer restroom. I bet someone is looking for you." Mr. Whitmore eyed her a moment longer before turning around. "Besides, you could get hurt back here," he said over his shoulder. "Follow me back up front."

Gracie wondered if her dad would be mad that she had wandered off. When she came back into the main part of the pharmacy, he was still waiting on his prescription. Gracie ran up to him and hoped Mr. Whitmore wouldn't say anything to him about her being in the back of the store. As luck would have it, someone asked for Mr. Whitmore's help behind the counter. He shuffled behind the counter, seemingly forgetting about the little blonde-headed nuisance who had been roaming around his business moments earlier.

Gracie let out a sigh of relief. That could have gone much worse.

"Did you find Mimi a gift?" her dad asked.

"Uh, sure." Gracie grabbed Mimi's favorite candy bar at the register. "She loves these."

Gracie's dad smiled. "She does have a sweet tooth."

Gracie tried to smile, but she was bummed that she hadn't found what the key opened. She racked her brain during the drive home to try to figure out where else she might look.

Out of nowhere, it came to her. Cassidy's house locks might be newer, but she never asked Cassidy if anything was left inside the house that might have that kind of lock on it.

***

The next morning, Gracie's mother dropped her off at Mimi's on her way to work at the hospital. Gracie presented Mimi with the candy bar she had bought at Whitmore's the night before.

"Bless you, Grace. That's my favorite. Thank you for thinking of me."

Gracie beamed. "I love you." She kissed Mimi's cheek.

After she ate breakfast, Gracie headed to Cassidy's house across the street. Cassidy's mom opened the door.

"Good morning! You must be Gracie." Mrs. Green had orange baby food on the left shoulder of her shirt. Gracie tried not to look at it as Mrs. Green invited her inside.

Other than a few boxes piled in the corner, the Greens had pretty much settled into their new home. It looked cozy and inviting.

Mr. Green was drinking his coffee and reading the paper. The baby sat in a high chair smiling with orange goop around his mouth, and Cassidy ate her cereal beside him.

As Cassidy washed her bowl out, Mr. Green put down his paper. "What are you girls going to get into today?"

"I don't know. Maybe just playing around here," said Cassidy.

"That's probably wise. It looks like it might rain," said Mrs. Green as she wiped at the baby's mouth.

"Do you want to see my room?" asked Cassidy.

"Sure," Gracie said, following Cassidy out of the dining room.

"Make sure to help your mom put away those last few boxes sometime today, Cass!" Mr. Green called from the dining room.

"I will!" Cassidy shut the door behind them. "The never-ending boxes. Dad starts work at the bank today."

Gracie looked around the room, impressed with how big and clean it was. Cassidy's bed was a pretty, white-metal daybed that served as a couch during the day. It was covered in pillows and stuffed animals of all kinds and colors.

Gracie wanted to jump and land right in the middle of it. They had decorated the room with butterflies and soothing shades of blue and green.

Cassidy also had the biggest dollhouse Gracie had ever seen. It was taller than Gracie! Gracie stepped closer to peer into each room of the dollhouse. Though she usually wasn't very interested in playing with dolls, she couldn't wait to play with the dollhouse.

"Okay, before I get sidetracked by this amazing dollhouse," Gracie said, pulling the key from her pocket, "I had an idea last night. You said the door locks in this house aren't a fit for skeleton keys, but what about something else that was left in the house? A big piece of furniture?"

"No, I don't think anything was left in the house. It was cleared out by the previous owners.

All the furniture here is from our old house—or it's new."

Gracie plopped down cross-legged on the plush gray carpet. "Oh, I give up. I guess it'll have to stay a mystery." She handed the brass key back to Cassidy, who put it on her nightstand.

Gracie and Cassidy played with Cassidy's dolls and the dollhouse for a while. Cassidy showed Gracie her collection of books, and they listened to some music that Cassidy liked. The music was by bands Gracie had never heard of, but she found the music interesting. Cassidy had even gone to the live concert of one of the bands they listened to. Gracie felt like Cassidy was so worldly for having grown up in the city. She had definitely had different experiences from Gracie's life in Loblolly.

Beckett poked his head into the room. "Hey, your mom sent me back here. Gracie, Mimi is asking if you're eating lunch. She told me to get you."

"Lunch!" Gracie looked down at her watch. "Wow, I didn't realize it was almost lunchtime. What have you been doing all morning?"

"I met up with some of the guys from my baseball team, and we practiced for an hour or so." Beckett played youth league baseball every summer, and Gracie loved going to the field to watch him play. "Let's go outside and swing before lunch. Or play tag." Beckett spied the key on the nightstand and picked it up. "Did you figure out what this went to, Gracie?"

"No. I went over to Whitmore Pharmacy last night, but there was nothing there that I could find."

"Too bad."

"Let me check with my mom about going out to play," Cassidy said. She peeked out the window. "It's cloudy but not raining yet. It should be Jameson's naptime soon, anyway." Cassidy left Beckett and Gracie in her room.

Gracie said, "I could play in this room forever."

Beckett looked around. "I don't see what's so great about it."

"Well, for one thing, look at the size of this dollhouse."

"You don't even play with dolls."

"I do sometimes," she said and picked up a doll as proof. "And there's so much room in here. It isn't messy like my room. Cassidy says she even has costumes in her closet we can play dress up in!"

Beckett's eyes seemed to light up at that, but then he said, "Eh, probably just princess dresses and girly stuff like that."

Cassidy came through the door just then with a big box in her hands. "Mom says I have to put these boxes in the attic before I can go out. Will you help me?"

"A creepy old attic on a stormy day? Why yes, sign me up!" Gracie said cheerfully as Beckett shrugged.

"I don't know about creepy. I haven't been up there yet, but Dad says it's safe to store some things there until we decide what we're going to do with the room. Mom wants to make it into an office, and Dad wants to make it into a home theater."

Gracie and Beckett each grabbed another box to take to the attic. The three kids climbed the narrow back stairs that led to a partially finished room above the first floor. The floor was finished in shiny hardwood, but the slanted ceiling still had exposed beams. The drywall was left unpainted and only about half-finished.

The kids set their boxes down and looked around the room in the dim light of the single attic bulb.

In addition to some boxes Mr. Green had added to the attic, there was an old kerosene heater and an ancient sewing machine lying on its side beside a pile of encyclopedias. It looked like only letters A through K were there. Beckett also found a dusty croquet set that he pulled out for them to play with in the backyard later.

"What's that?" Gracie pointed to a huge rectangular box at the end of the attic.

"I don't know. I've never seen it before," said Cassidy. They ran over to take a closer look and realized it was an old trunk.

"Could it be the lock that our skeleton key fits into?" Gracie smiled with excitement, her eyes wide.

Gracie raced downstairs to grab the key. Beckett and Cassidy stayed in the attic to inspect the outside of the trunk. Beckett was pulling up on the top when Gracie returned to the attic. The trunk's top wouldn't budge an inch. Gracie held up the key, panting from the sprint back up the stairs.

"Give me a hand," Beckett said to Cassidy, and the two slid it forward away from the wall. "Whatever is in it is heavy."

"That's probably why it's still up here," said Cassidy. "Nobody wanted to move this big ol' thing. What do you think is in it?"

Beckett's eyes widened. "Maybe it's a treasure chest full of gold doubloons."

"Doubloons? Have you been reading pirate books again, Beckett?" Gracie laughed. "Surely, no one would leave a chest full of gold coins up here."

Gracie handed the skeleton key to Cassidy. Cassidy slid the key into the lock, turned it to the left, and heard it click as the lock released.

"Amazing!" cried Gracie.

Chapter 6

"Open it up!" said Beckett. He grabbed one side of the top, and Gracie grabbed the other. They pulled it up and peered into the trunk.

Cassidy whispered, "What is it? What's in it?"

"It isn't treasure," said Gracie, "or at least not gold. I guess it might still be considered a treasure." She pulled out a couple of old patchwork quilts and laid them on the floor. "Hey, there's a picture album in here." Gracie pulled out a large blue album and handed it to Beckett. The album was thick and heavy, full of pictures and memories of another time.

Beckett opened it. Many of the photos had turned red and orange with age or were in black and white.

"What else is in here?" asked Gracie, as she peered into the trunk. There was a striped scarf, a dainty red handbag, and several old books. She pulled out a family Bible, which was even thicker than the photo album. There was also a silk corsage in a plastic bag. "I can't believe someone left all this stuff up here. It seems like it would be important to whoever put them here. Don't you think?"

"I agree. But if the key was lost and the family couldn't get into the trunk, they might've just left it," Cassidy said.

"The key wasn't lost. It was hidden," Gracie corrected her.

"Right," said Cassidy. "I almost forgot."

"But why did they hide it?" Gracie wondered.

"Good question," Beckett added, flipping through the photo album in his lap. "And if it was buried, maybe this trunk was left on purpose. To be forgotten. Hey!" He pointed to a photo. "Isn't this Mimi?"

"Yes! I recognize her. She's so young in that picture. I can't believe she's a part of our mystery." Gracie stared at the fading photo of several young adults leaning against an old pickup truck. Mimi's curly hair was much longer and parted down the middle, and she wore a striped shirt and wide-leg jeans. She looked to be twenty years old or maybe a little older. Gracie smiled at the picture. "Amazing! She was really gorgeous."

"I wonder who these other people in the picture are," said Beckett.

"I've been thinking," said Cassidy. "Maybe someone buried the key because something in here was too difficult to deal with—or it made them too sad. So, maybe they buried the key to keep themselves from opening this back up over and over again. Maybe." Cassidy wrinkled her nose and frowned as if she were unsure of her own guess about the trunk.

"I could see that," said Gracie. "It's basically what I do with my homework when I can't bring myself to look at it anymore," she joked.

Gracie flipped through the Bible. There was an intricate family tree chart at the beginning. She could barely read the faded cursive writing in the low light, though she had just learned to write and read in cursive this past school year. Besides, she really didn't know how to read all the lines of the family tree chart anyway. It looked like a strange maze.

As she flipped pages, something fell out. Cassidy picked it up and turned it over in her hands. It was a small envelope containing an invitation. The name Brian was written in cursive on the front. The envelope was unsealed as if it had never been closed, so Gracie pulled out the invitation. It featured two birds and flowers, and it announced the wedding ceremony of Keith Nash and Jacqueline Whitmore. The wedding date was from 1979.

"Check this out," Gracie said, pointing to the invitation. "Someone named Jacqueline Whitmore left her wedding invitation in the trunk. Maybe the wooden box and key were hers?"

Beckett put down the album. "Maybe so. I wonder what, if any connection, she has to the pharmacist."

Gracie handed him the Bible. "See if you can make heads or tails out of that family tree in the front of the Bible. I can't read the writing."

Beckett examined the family tree. "I can see the Whitmore name several times, but no, it's too hard to read." He closed the Bible. "Have you gotten everything out of the trunk?"

Gracie peered into the dark trunk. "No, there's something else in there." Tucked into the corner and almost hidden in the gloom was a small golden locket on a dainty chain. Gracie held it in the palm of her hand to show the others. The locket was oval with flowers engraved on the front. The back of the locket was smooth. "Amazing! We did find treasure."

"It's pretty," said Cassidy.

"See what's inside it," said Beckett.

Gracie gently pried open the locket with her thumbnail. Two photos faced each other—a young man and a young woman.

"Do you think these two were sweethearts or maybe married?" asked Cassidy.

Gracie studied the pictures. The man looked familiar. Where had she seen him? The eyes. She had seen those piercing gray eyes before. She frowned.

"Beckett, doesn't this man look familiar to you?"

"Maybe..." Beckett pulled the photo album back into his lap and began flipping through pages. "Look at this one with Mimi that we found. The girl and boy there, that's the two from the locket. And here's one where they are at the beach. They're much younger, but that's them." He flipped back a few pages. "Here's another where the boy is having a birthday party. He looks to be our age here, but that's him." Beckett pointed to a little girl in the picture. "And that's her."

"You're right! Either these two have known each other from childhood, or they're family."

Cassidy looked closely at the images in the locket. "They do look alike. Same hair color, similar noses. They could be family."

"If they grew up in Loblolly, it shouldn't be hard to figure out who they are," said Beckett.

"Besides, Mimi is in this album, so surely she remembers them. Let's take the album and locket to her," Gracie said, her voice rising with anticipation.

Chapter 7

The three friends entered the cool living room across the street looking for Mimi. They went all through the house and then out the back door. They found her in the backyard trimming her roses and humming to herself.

"Hello, kids. What are you up to on this cloudy day?" Mimi looked up as if expecting rain. She snipped off a rose that had faded and was losing petals. "Ready for some lunch?"

"We need your help. We found a key that opened a trunk and a locket that has two photos of people we also found in an album. We even saw you in the album. We think the man looks familiar and wanted to see if you remembered them," Gracie said in a rush.

"Goodness! You *have* been busy. It's only 11 o'clock!" Mimi smiled and took the locket from Cassidy. "Well, this does take me back. These two were sister and brother, the closest pair you would ever know. The man is familiar to you because that is Brian Whitmore."

"Mr. Whitmore! I knew I had seen those eyes." Gracie remembered him peering down at her in the back of the pharmacy. She shuddered at the memory.

"These were taken many years ago when they were still in school." Mimi handed the locket back to Cassidy. "Wherever did you find this?"

"In my house," said Cassidy.

"There was an old trunk in their attic with these things and some other stuff, too."

Mimi took the album from Beckett's hands and sat down on the little wrought-iron bench beside her massive rose bushes. A bee buzzed near her head, but she was already flipping through the pictures and didn't notice it. A hint of a smile twitched at her lips as she examined each picture.

"Yes, there I am. I remember that day well. We had all gone fishing at Bell Farm Creek." Mimi smiled, remembering. "Brian and his best friend Keith pushed each other into the water, goofing around. Before long, we were all taking a swim in the creek. That was one of the hottest summers I can remember. We were all just teenagers back then."

"I can't imagine a summer hotter than this one," Gracie said.

"Oh, but it was." Mimi's smiling face clouded over. "That was before."

"Before what?" Beckett asked.

"Before our whole group of friends broke up. Before Brian and his sister, Jackie, had the falling out, and everyone took sides."

"Jackie... Jacqueline Whitmore?" asked Cassidy.

"And Keith," whispered Beckett. "From the wedding invitation."

"Yes, but we called her Jackie."

"Sounds interesting! Tell us what happened, Mimi," said Gracie.

Mimi closed the album. "I had almost forgotten that Jackie lived in the house across the street. She only lived there a short time. Brian and Jackie, as I said, were very close. They were more like best friends than like brother and sister. Jackie was only a year younger than him. We were all friends from school. Brian and Jackie grew up in that yellow two-story house just down the road from the pharmacy. I think Brian owns now. You know the one? That pharmacy has always been the family business. Both Brian and Jackie worked there as teenagers. Oh, the many milkshakes I remember having there as I visited them.

"Anyway, I digress. Jackie and Keith Nash started dating. Though Brian and Keith were best friends, Brian didn't think Keith was good enough for his little sister. He was very protective of her. That was what split the whole group apart. Some took Brian's side, and others took Jackie's side. Soon, Brian told Jackie that if she and Keith got serious, he would disown her."

"Like stop being her brother?" Gracie asked. Her mouth hung open in dismay.

"Yes."

"That's awful!" cried Gracie.

"A love story?" Beckett rolled his eyes.

"It's a story about family and friendships broken. Not just love, Beckett."

"Yep, Brian was passionate about it—and stubborn. I'm not really sure what he had against Keith—just that he didn't think Keith was right for his little sister. Jackie was stubborn, too. And when Keith and Jackie announced that they were getting married, Brian wouldn't have anything to do with her or his best friend." She closed the album. "Keith and Jackie briefly rented the house across the street after they married. Then, they moved away from here. As far as I know, she never came back to Loblolly."

"So they still don't speak to each other?"

"I don't think so. I'm not sure. I haven't talked to either of them in a long time," Mimi said, still frowning.

"All those years of missed memories." Gracie frowned. She and Beckett were close like Mr.

Whitmore and his sister had been. She couldn't imagine anything or anyone making her and Beckett never speak to each other again. She could see Jackie locking away her memories and burying that key in the wooden box under the Oak before she said goodbye to Loblolly and the life she had known here. How terrible that must have felt. She sighed. The whole story made her sad.

The mystery of the wooden box was turning out to be not-so-amazing after all.

Chapter 8

"Shhhh," said Cassidy. Gracie snickered again. Beckett was "it," and she knew he would find their hiding places soon. He was good at the game. Hide and seek made her giddy, and it bubbled up into giggles that she couldn't seem to help.

Gracie heard the stairs creak as Beckett came off the front porch of Mimi's house. She slapped one hand over her mouth to keep from giggling while holding onto the tree branch with the other hand.

While Gracie had quickly climbed a tree with low branches beside Mimi's house, Cassidy had hidden just off the right side of the porch behind a big bushy pampas grass plant. The plant was almost as tall as the house. Because it was so wide, it offered a great hiding spot, especially if the person would brave the sharp grass blades and settle in under them. Cassidy had only partially burrowed into the grass before Beckett had yelled, "Ready or not, here I come!"

Gracie peered down at her and could see Cassidy's legs sticking out from under the pampas. She almost giggled again.

Beckett came into view around the house, and Gracie hoped he wouldn't look up. If he did, he would see her right away. She was right above his head. She stayed very still and held her breath. He walked under the tree, and she felt relieved. He would surely see Cassidy first.

At that moment, Hugo came racing around the house, stopped below Gracie, pawed at the trunk, and yapped at her. Gracie tried to motion him away with her hand, but Hugo had already gotten Beckett's attention. He spied Gracie in the tree, a huge smile spreading across his face. He tugged at her leg. "Gotcha!"

"Aw, Hugo!" said Gracie. She hopped down off the low branch and crossed her arms. "That's not fair. You got help from the dog."

"Now, let me see where—Aha! Found you, Cassidy."

Cassidy peeked from underneath the pampas grass and came out of hiding.

"Gracie is it. I found her first," Beckett said.

"I'm tired of this game," Gracie complained. "We've already played five rounds, and it's hot as blue blazes out here." She wiped the sweat from her forehead.

"We could go in and watch some TV," suggested Beckett.

"There's nothing good on. Do you think we would disturb Jameson if we played over at your house?" Gracie asked.

"He should be up from his nap," said Cassidy.

"Great! I'd love to play in your dollhouse again."

"The dollhouse?" moaned Beckett. "I'm going in to watch TV. No way am I playing in a dollhouse."

"Okay, see you later, Beckett," said Gracie.

Beckett trudged up the front steps, looking over his shoulder as Gracie and Cassidy crossed the street, led by Hugo.

In Cassidy's room, the girls played with dolls for a little while, and then Cassidy's mom peeked her head into the room. "Would you two like to help me make cookies?"

"Sure!" they exclaimed in unison and jumped up to follow Mrs. Green into the kitchen.

Jameson crawled around in his playpen in the living room, which they could see from the table. The girls sat down as Cassidy's mother placed all the ingredients on the table in front of them. "We're making sugar cookies. You can cut them into shapes and even decorate them if you want to."

For a moment, Gracie felt guilty that Beckett was missing this fun. He would love decorating cookies. "May I decorate one to take to Beckett later?"

"Sure. You can make several to take home. Make sure to decorate one for your grandmother, too, if you think Mrs. Nancy might like one."

"Oh, she'll love that. Thanks."

Cassidy stirred the ingredients together that Mrs. Green added to the bowl. Once the dough was mixed well, Gracie rolled it out on the floured surface Mrs. Green had prepared. Then, the girls chose the cookie cutters they liked and began cutting out cookies. Gracie chose a heart for herself, a star for Beckett, and a flower for Mimi. She nibbled on a piece of cookie dough while Cassidy finished cutting out cookie shapes.

"What do we have for decorations?" asked Gracie.

"We have a couple of different kinds of sprinkles and a few different colors of cookie icing." Mrs. Green pulled the decorations out and placed them on the table. "So Cassidy tells me you kids found a bit of treasure here the other day."

"Yes, but it turned out to be a not-so-happy ending to our mystery."

"Cassidy told me the story about the pharmacist and his sister. That's too bad. You could ask him how his sister is doing. It might give you an idea of whether they ever made up over the years." She winked and grinned. "Maybe your mystery hasn't quite ended." Mrs. Green carried the bowl to the sink.

"That's true," Gracie murmured. She wasn't sure she had the courage to ask Mr. Whitmore about his sister, though. He seemed a little scary. Would he yell at her for bringing up bad memories?

"Maybe giving them their stuff back would make them remember how wonderful their relationship was before they had the falling out," said Cassidy. "Or like Mom says, they could have already made up."

"His sister probably wants the old trunk back after all these years. That might be the reason you could talk to him about it. It's rightfully theirs," added Mrs. Green as she shooed the girls into the living room to play so she could clean up the flour and bits of dough while the cookies baked.

The way Jackie had hidden the key made Gracie think that she never wanted to see its contents again. It wouldn't hurt to ask, though, she guessed. Jackie could have had a change of heart after all these years.

The girls played with Jameson while they waited for the cookies to bake and to cool. Once they were cooled, Mrs. Green called the girls back to the table to decorate them.

Gracie smeared her heart cookie with lime green and purple icing. Then, she decorated it with pink sprinkles. It looked almost too pretty to eat. She iced Beckett's star with yellow icing and added rainbow sprinkles to it. On Mimi's cookie, she iced the flower petals with pink icing and put a bit of yellow icing in the center. She added a few chocolate sprinkles to the center. Gracie admired her work. "These are amazing!"

She and Cassidy decided to eat the ones they had made for themselves. The cookies were soft and yummy. Gracie couldn't wait to share the ones she decorated for Beckett and Mimi.

Chapter 9

After Gracie said goodbye to Cassidy, Jameson, and Mrs. Green, she headed back to Mimi's with her cookies on a paper plate. She found Beckett snoring softly on the couch, the TV tuned to a baseball game. She let him sleep and pulled out a stool at the bar where Mimi was working a word-search puzzle and drinking coffee.

Gracie presented Mimi with the flower cookie. She fussed over how pretty it was and put it up to eat later. She helped Mimi find a few words in the puzzle before she went back to the couch to give Beckett his cookie. Gracie was excited to see how pleased he would be with the yummy treat she had worked so hard on.

"Wake up, Beckett." She poked him in the side.

Beckett opened his eyes, turned away from her, and said, "Leave me alone."

"What's got you in such a foul mood? Did you have a bad dream?"

"No."

"I brought you something," Gracie said with a proud smile.

"I don't want it, whatever it is."

"But it's a delicious cookie," she said, holding the plate near his head.

He turned back over. "Where did you get it?"

"I made it at Cassidy's. I decorated it for you, too. It's a yellow star, and I put-"

"I don't want it," he interrupted.

"Beckett, what's wrong?" Gracie asked.

She already knew what was wrong, though. He was jealous of her friendship with Cassidy. She had been sensing it for days in the way his shoulders slumped when she mentioned Cassidy or by the way he seemed discouraged when Gracie wanted to hang out at Cassidy's. Gracie tried to include Beckett as much as she could, but sometimes, the girls wanted to play with things Beckett wasn't interested in, like the dollhouse or playing salon with hair bows and nail polish.

He turned back over. "I'm going back to sleep."

"You don't need sleep. You need this delicious cookie—and you need to talk to me."

"You have Cassidy to talk to."

"Beckett, don't be like that.

"Like what?" he grumbled and looked away.

"I like doing girl stuff with Cassidy, the stuff you don't care about. And we both like hanging out with her. She's nice and fun to play with. But *you* are my cousin. You are the closest thing I have to a brother. No one can compare to that. Ever."

At that moment, Gracie could see how easily someone's feelings could get hurt over friendships and misunderstandings. She felt sorry all over again for Mr. Whitmore and his sister. Had they ever been able to forgive and forget? Mimi said that family was the most important thing in the world, and Gracie believed that she was right.

"Besides," she added, "I bet once you get busy with summer baseball games, you won't even mind that I go over to Cassidy's to play sometimes."

"We are playing more games now that school is out." Beckett sat up, tucked his socked feet under his legs, and eyed the cookie on the plate. "It *is* a nice cookie."

Gracie handed him the plate. "And delicious, too!" She sat down beside him and watched the baseball game on the television while he gobbled up his treat.

He wiped crumbs off his cheek with his wrist. "That was..." he began, and they both said, "AMAZING!" and burst into laughter.

"Okay, Cassidy's mom brought up a good point today while we were making cookies," said Gracie. "Maybe our mystery isn't solved yet."

"It's seemed pretty much over to me."

"What if they forgave each other? In which case, we should get their stuff back to them. Even if they didn't forgive each other, I bet Mrs. Jackie would like the stuff back now. It's been such a long time. Who knows? Seeing these old memories could make her want to make up with her brother. If they're still at odds, shouldn't we try to help them? It's worth a try, right?"

"Yes, it is worth a try," he agreed. "They're family."

"Good. Let's go over to the pharmacy and talk to Mr. Whitmore. I bet Mimi would take us if she knew why we wanted to go. And I wouldn't mind having her around in case Mr. Whitmore gets angry about the things left in the trunk," said Gracie.

"Let's go ask her—and let's see if Cassidy can go with us. We *did* find it at her house."

Gracie smiled. "Good idea, Beckett."

86

Chapter 10

Luckily, Mimi wasn't opposed to the idea of talking to Mr. Whitmore, though she cautioned, "Don't be disappointed if he tells you to get lost. It's really none of our business, even though you're trying to do a good thing here. Just remember that he may not see it that way."

Mrs. Green had gotten to know Gracie's grandmother a little over the few weeks since they had moved in. She gave Cassidy permission to ride over to the pharmacy with them. The three buckled themselves into the back of Mimi's SUV. Since Mimi had grown up with Mr. Whitmore, Gracie felt more confident about talking to him.

Cassidy brought along the wooden box, which held the skeleton key. Beckett held the photo album of pictures in his lap. Gracie held the locket in her hand, hoping that seeing it would flood Mr. Whitmore with fond memories of his sister—instead of the bad memories that had torn them apart. The three walked into the pharmacy with Mimi leading the way, her flowery dress fluttering behind her.

Mimi asked for Mr. Whitmore, but the woman behind the desk said that he was at home. It turned out to be his day off.

"Oh, no." Gracie's shoulders slumped.

Cassidy frowned. Beckett even looked frustrated. They had seemed to hit another dead-end in their quest to solve the mystery of the wooden box.

Mimi ushered the kids onto the sidewalk when she saw their glum faces. "Chin up, kids. Don't give up so easily." She turned and took off down the sidewalk.

"Wait! Where's she going?" Beckett asked.

Gracie followed her, saying over her shoulder, "Mr. Whitmore's house is just down the street."

Cassidy and Beckett's faces lit up, and they quickly followed.

The two-story yellow house was only a short walk from the pharmacy. The four of them stood at the door as Mimi knocked. Gracie listened but didn't hear anyone coming. Mimi knocked again. Gracie had all but given up on anyone answering the door when she finally saw a figure through the colored glass in the middle of the door.

Mr. Whitmore pulled open the door wide, a look of surprise on his face which replaced the usual frown that Gracie remembered.

"I don't need any cookies—or magazines, either," he said.

There was the frown Gracie had come to know.

"Brian Whitmore, we aren't here to sell you anything," Mimi said with a grin.

"Nancy!" he said, using Mimi's real name. "Nancy, it has been a very long time. I almost didn't recognize you. What can I do for you?"

"Well, my grandchildren Beckett and Grace, and their friend Cassidy, have found something in her house that they want you to see." Mimi paused, but when he didn't invite them in, she asked, "May we come in for a bit, Brian?"

"Oh," he raked his hand through his white hair. "Of course. Come in." He ushered them into his formal parlor, a stuffy, uncomfortable room that looked like no one ever ventured into. The kids sat down on a hard, antique sofa that had seen better days, and Mimi sat in a green chair by an old piano.

Mr. Whitmore didn't sit. He leaned against the door frame and crossed his arms. "I don't get many visitors."

Mimi looked at Gracie and nodded.

Gracie took a big gulp of air and said, "Mr. Whitmore, we found some things that we believe belonged to your sister, Jackie, who Mimi told us a little about." She paused to see how he would react to the mention of his sister.

He was stoic, his face showing no emotion at all.

"There was an old trunk left in Cassidy's attic where Jackie lived for a while before leaving Loblolly," Gracie continued. "You see, we found the key to the trunk buried in the backyard, which we found a little odd, and your last name was on the bottom of the wooden box we found it in."

"Is that why you came snooping around my pharmacy the other day?"

"Yes, sir," she admitted. She noticed that Mimi raised her eyebrows. "I wondered if the key opened anything there. Sorry about that."

Beckett said, "Gracie wanted to solve the mystery of the wooden box. We couldn't understand why someone would want to bury a key."

"I wouldn't have opened something at your business without talking to you first about it," Gracie said. "I was just trying to find something that it could possibly open. We weren't sure at that point that the key had anything to do with you, though. We only had a name on the bottom of the box." Cassidy lifted the box so Mr. Whitmore could see the letters carved into the wood.

"When we found the trunk in my attic and realized it had a skeleton-key lock, we opened it," said Cassidy. "We realized these were items that someone might want back, so we went to Mrs. Nancy to find out where we could find the people they belonged to."

"We found that picture album," Gracie pointed to the album Beckett still held in his hands, "and this locket. Mimi recognized you and Jackie. We wondered if you might want to get in touch with her or give us her phone number so we can let her know that we have her things." Gracie looked at him hopefully and smiled.

Mr. Whitmore came over to Gracie and took the locket from her hands. He turned it over, rubbing the roses on the front with his thumb. He gently opened the locket and looked at the photos of himself and his sister from so long ago. The hint of a smile played on his lips. "Yes, this was hers," he whispered. He laid it back into Gracie's hand.

"Brian," said Mimi gently. "Where is Jackie now?"

Mr. Whitmore looked up with sadness in his eyes. Gracie dreaded the worst—that they had never made amends and would never be able to.

"I'm right here."

Chapter 11

Everyone turned to the doorway of the parlor, and there stood an aging, plump version of the young woman in the locket that Gracie held.

It was Jackie!

Gracie, Beckett, and Cassidy sat on the sofa with eyes wide and mouths open. Gracie looked at Mimi, who was also surprised.

"I can't believe it!" Mimi said. She got up and hugged Jackie. "It's wonderful to see you after all these years."

"I've been meaning to visit you, Nancy. Forgive me." Mrs. Jackie smiled.

Mimi waved away the apology with her hand. "Oh, it's alright. I'm just glad to see you now. And here!" Mimi glanced at Mr. Whitmore.

"Mrs. Jackie," Gracie said as she stood up and handed the lady her locket. "This is yours."

"Oh, thank you, dear! I haven't seen this in so many years." Jackie opened it up to look at the pictures inside. "I heard your story as I finished making tea, and I am so thankful that you were able to solve the mystery. I would love to have my things back that I left behind in that attic. In anger and frustration, I tried to forget how much I loved my brother. I left those memories behind there. It was a very poor choice—one that I regret so much."

"We both did and said regrettable things," said Mr. Whitmore.

"But I am thankful that you kids worked so hard to return the possessions. One question, though," said Mrs. Jackie. "How did you find the wooden box to begin with? I seem to remember burying it in the yard somewhere."

"Yes," Cassidy said with a smile. "We have my little dog Hugo to thank for that. He found the box under that big Oak in the backyard."

"I see. Well, to answer the question that is on everyone's mind, Brian and I did finally forgive each other. We were very hard-headed in our younger years.

"Neither of us wanted to swallow our pride. We forgot how important family was until too many years had passed," said Mr. Whitmore.

"Brian reached out to me and my husband Keith a few years ago and invited us all to Christmas here at my parent's old house. Our families have reconciled."

"Now, she comes around every moment she can to bug me," Mr. Whitmore said with a grin. "We usually spend my day off from the pharmacy catching up and talking about old times."

Mrs. Jackie went to the kitchen and brought out tea for everyone. They all sat around the parlor looking through photos in the picture album while Mimi, Brian, and Jackie told stories of the old days.

Gracie looked at Beckett, who was laughing with Cassidy about their adventure. Gracie vowed to never take her cousin or her other friendships for granted. Mimi laughed as Mr. Whitmore told a story about his first time driving. Mimi had lost so many years of good memories as the friendships she had made as a child broke apart. Family and friendships were important.

The Mystery of the Wooden Box

Gracie twirled the brass skeleton key in her hand. If the mystery of the wooden box had taught her anything, it was that burying or locking away bad feelings and memories wasn't the way to solve problems with family and friends.

The keys to good relationships were open conversations, honesty, and forgiveness. When Beckett was jealous of her new friendship with Cassidy, they had to be honest with each other and talk about the issue instead of ignoring the problem. Gracie knew that she would always work hard to let the important people in her life know that she loved them.

Want even more **Amazing Gracie Mysteries**? Read the first chapter of the next book in the series **The Eerie Beach Light** here.

The Eerie Beach Light

Chapter 1

G racie glanced at the car's GPS, wondering if
they were almost to Sand Dollar Beach. Rain

drummed on the car's roof as her mom hunched forward over the steering wheel, trying to see through the spattering rain and the frantic back and forth swoosh of wipers across the windshield. Her dad snored in the seat in front of her.

"How many hours have we been driving?" Gracie asked. She tried not to sound like she was complaining, but she was tired of sitting in the car. She needed to move. She wiggled around in her seat to get more comfortable. It didn't really help.

"Including stopping for lunch, we've been in the car eight and a half hours now," her mom said, looking at Gracie in the rearview mirror. "Need another pit stop?"

"No, not yet. If we're close, just keep going. I'm ready to see the ocean."

"We're not far now," her mom replied.

Gracie nearly hopped in her seat with excitement. They would be there soon! She leaned forward and tugged at her dad's hair to wake him up.

He sat forward and wiped at his eyes. "How long has it been raining?"

"About thirty minutes," Gracie's mom said.

Gracie glanced at her cousin Beckett, who ignored the rain as he read a comic book. She looked up at the dark sky and sighed. It was supposed to be sunny. She hoped this rain wasn't a forewarning of what the rest of their beach vacation was going to be like. She had waited so long for this trip. Gracie picked up her tablet. "My weather app says the thunderstorm is right over us," Gracie told her dad. A streak of lightning and a quick crack of thunder followed, confirming the weather report.

"Just a little summer thunderstorm. Nothing to worry about," he said.

"Hey, Beckett. The GPS says we're almost to our turn off for the coast," Gracie said. "Why don't you get your nose out of that comic and see some scenery?"

Beckett grumbled but laid it down and looked out his window. "What scenery? It's just cars passing us down the interstate, a bunch of trees, and rain." He had been moody the entire trip, and Gracie was worried that he wouldn't have any fun during their family vacation. He created his own little, dark cloud.

The GPS signaled to take the next exit. They turned onto a road that took them through a small, southern coastal town. The rain slacked off to a fine mist, and the sky lightened a little from the dark gloom.

Beckett stared out his window.

Gracie was excited to see the ocean, but so far, the towns they passed through looked similar to the town they lived in, Loblolly. Gracie leaned forward. "Are we there yet?" She grinned when her mother gave her a sideways glance.

"No, we've got two more towns to go through before we get to Sand Dollar Beach. Just sit back and relax. It'll be another half hour. Maybe more, depending on traffic."

Gracie sighed and plopped back into her seat. She realized that driving to their destination was her least favorite part of vacation. It was even worse than packing. She popped a bubble-gum bubble, blew another one—this one way bigger—and leaned over to show Beckett. "Unh!" She pointed at her massive purple bubble, her eyes wide. She thumped Beckett on the arm when he didn't notice.

He turned around, a smile playing on his lips, and stuck his finger in the bubble. It popped and went all over her nose and chin.

"Hey!" she said but laughed as she picked gum off her face.

Beckett grinned.

Gracie thought it was probably the first time she'd seen him smile since they left Loblolly. "That was the biggest bubble I've ever made. Wasn't it amazing?"

He gazed past her. "Look, I see a palm tree." He pointed out the window at a large palm in someone's front yard. "And the beach!" He sat up in his seat as they all gazed between houses, catching glimpses of the white sand and a stormy sea beyond it. As stormy as the sky was above the dark emerald water, the ocean still looked breathtakingly beautiful.

Gracie could stare at the ocean all day.

Lightning zigzagged down to the ocean from the rolling clouds, and she gasped. "Wow."

"Now, that's amazing," Beckett said.

***

Their first night in Sand Dollar Beach, a constant drizzling rain confined them to the beach house. Uncle Lee, Beckett's dad, ordered pizzas from a local place, and everyone dug in.

"This has got to be the best bacon pizza I've ever had!" Gracie exclaimed as she grabbed a second slice.

"I agree," said Beckett, letting a long string of melted cheese fall into his open mouth. "Extra cheesy."

After they ate, Gracie's mom and dad proposed a game of cards. Gracie, Beckett, and Beckett's older sister Harper joined in while Uncle Lee and Stella, his new fiancée, settled down on the couch to watch a movie. They ended up playing five rounds of Go Fish and three rounds of Rummy.

"Okay, kids, it's past bedtime," Gracie's mom said as she gathered up the cards to put back into the box.

"Aw!" Gracie whined. She threw her last hand into the pile. Though she didn't feel like going to bed, her eyes were heavy. Actually, her whole body felt weighed down. Maybe she did need some sleep.

Beckett grumbled, "Not like I'm winning anyway." He threw down his hand, glanced at his dad and Stella, who were still watching the movie, and got up from the table. "Beat you to the bathroom," Beckett said as he sped past Gracie.

"Hey!" Gracie jumped up from her seat, ran after Beckett, and reached the door as it closed.

"Come on," Harper said. "We can go to the one upstairs. Let's find pajamas, and I'll brush your hair." Harper didn't have a little sister, so she always wanted to play with Gracie's hair or paint her nails, and Gracie loved the attention. Gracie didn't have siblings, but she was lucky to have close cousins like

Beckett and Harper. Gracie noticed the rain had stopped. It was quieter, but she could now hear the sound of the ocean, which made her want to go out to the beach even more.

After she changed into pajamas, Gracie sat cross legged on the bed while Harper took down her braided hair and brushed it out. It fell down in a cascade of blonde waves.

"My mom used to call waves from my hair being braided all day my 'mermaid hair,'" Harper said softly.

Gracie liked that. The ripples did look like what she would imagine a mermaid's hair would be. Gracie could barely remember her aunt, and she wondered if the memory of Harper's mother unbraiding her hair made Harper sad. It made Gracie a little sad for her.

"Okay, Goldie Locks," Harper said as she laid the brush on the nightstand, "it's your turn for the bathroom." She yawned and climbed up the ladder to the top bunk. "Turn the light out?"

Gracie flipped the switch and then tiptoed to Beckett's room to see if he was still up. She imagined he would be up reading his comic book, but his light was off, and he was already snoring softly. "'Night, Beckett," she whispered.

She went into the bathroom with her toothbrush and paste. The house was silent when she exited the bathroom. Gracie supposed everyone was tired from the drive down to Florida, but all she could think about was going to the beach. Gracie tiptoed to her bedroom window and looked out to see if she could see the ocean. The moon peeked through clouds. A light far down the beach swung back and forth. Gracie wondered what it could be. Maybe a lighthouse. Or she guessed it could be car lights. It was hard to tell in the darkness where the beach ended and the streets began.

She gazed out her window a moment longer, taking in the beauty of the white sand illuminated by the moonlight, and then she snuggled into her bunk bed. Harper, above her, was already breathing deeply. As tired as Gracie was, she wasn't accustomed to this mattress and pillow or the sound of the ocean nearby, and she tossed back and forth. She flopped over and looked through the window. The clouds were gone now, and the stars twinkled in the dark sky. Gracie closed her eyes and drifted off to sleep.

Want to read more

AMAZING GRACIE MYSTERIES?

Visit CSCShows.com

Made in the USA
Middletown, DE
29 August 2021